MONKEY WITH A TOOL BELT AND THE CRAFTIEST CHRISTMAS EVER!

Chris Monroe

CAROLRHODA BOOKS MINNEAPOLIS

To Mom and Selah, our Christmas
Queen and Princess,

and to Dad, the Tinsel King

Carolrhoda Books®
An imprint of Lerner Publishing Group, Inc.
241 First Avenue North
Minneapolis, MN 55401 USA

For reading levels and more information, look up this title at www.lernerbooks.com.

Designed by Danielle Carnito.
Main body text set in Blockhead OT Unplugged. Typeface provided by Emigre, Inc.
The illustrations in this book were created in gouache, ink, and graphite on cold press
illustration board.

Library of Congress Cataloging-in-Publication Data

Names: Monroe, Chris, author, illustrator.
Title: Monkey with a tool belt and the craftiest Christmas ever! / Chris Monroe.
Description: Minneapolis, MN : Carolrhoda Books, [2021] | Audience: Ages 4–8. | Audience: Grades K–1.
   | Summary: With the help of his trusty tool belt, Chico Bon Bon helps friends decorate, turns a pile
   of junk into a bundle of gifts, and throws an epically awesome party.
Identifiers: LCCN 2021000724 (print) | LCCN 2021000725 (ebook) | ISBN 9781728404653 (trade
   hardcover) | ISBN 9781728430591 (ebook)
Subjects: CYAC: Monkeys—Fiction. | Animals—Fiction. | Tools—Fiction. | Christmas—Fiction.
Classification: LCC PZ7.M760 Moh 2021 (print) | LCC PZ7.M760 (ebook) | DDC [E]—dc23

LC record available at https://lccn.loc.gov/2021000724
LC ebook record available at https://lccn.loc.gov/2021000725

Manufactured in the United States of America
1-48525-49036-2/8/2021

It was just three days until
Chico Bon Bon's Christmas Party.

WHEEEEEE!

He and Clark were taking a break
from decorating to go sledding.

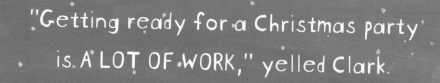

"Getting ready for a Christmas party is. A LOT OF WORK," yelled Clark.

Just then, the runner broke off his sled and he skidded partway down Marshmallow Hill.

SNAP!

SWOOSH

I'll fix it!

Chico reached for his tool belt.

Chico had all the tools a monkey
would ever need in the winter.

candy hammer

fruitcake saw

stocking crammer

extra paw

present shaker

snowball maker

wrapping ripper

cookie gripper

holly clipper

ice nipper

spritzy

bling blaster

ribbon twirler

Santa sensor

cocoa swirler

toy clamps

glitter buster

sugar plumb bob

star duster

candy cane

Soon they were zooming down the hill into the forest below.

At the bottom, they spotted a big shape covered in snow.

"Check out this ice monster, it's completely buried!" yelled Clark.

"Hey . . . wait a minute . . . it's a pile of JUNK!"

"That's peculiar," said Chico, brushing off more snow. "I wonder who would leave something like this in the woods!"

"We'd better haul this out of here," said Chico.

They piled all the junk on their sleds and began the slow hike back to Chico's treehouse.

"Let's just put it all in my work shed for now," said Chico. "I can bring it to the dump later. I have to help some friends first."

"Sounds good, Chico," said Clark. "I'm going Christmas shopping with my grandma. Later, I'll bring some candy cane muffins for the party."

"Hmm, shopping," thought Chico. "I almost forgot! I still have to get MY gifts for everyone!"

Chico spent that afternoon
helping friends. While he worked,
he thought about what he could
give them all for Christmas.

He strung up
some holiday lights
for the chickens.

Fixed the door
for the dogs'
diorama of Dickens.

Built a scratching post tree
for the kitty cat crew.

Hung a wreath
made of cheese
for the mice in a shoe.

On the way home, Chico wondered if
Clark was having a good time shopping.

When was **HE** going to find time to get gifts?

Early the next morning, Chico made cocoa and headed
out to the shed to sort through the junk pile.

It was an odd collection.

Some of it was pretty nice.

He drank his cocoa and thought about all the things in the pile.

Suddenly Chico had an idea. He could use the
junk to make presents for his friends!

He got right to work.

① He would need some privacy.

② He examined each piece and got some good ideas.

③ He did some wiring.

④ He deconstructed!

⑤ Then he constructed. He used a lot of his tools.

⑥ He sawed a bit of lumber.

⑦ It was noisy!

⑧ He worked late into the night.

⑨ It was time to get some sleep.

The next morning, Chico was awakened by the phone. It was Clark.

"Thanks," said Chico. "I will see you at the party!"

Chico hung up the phone and carried some wrapping paper and tape into the work shed.

He put the finishing touches on all the gifts.

When Chico woke up the next morning, his first thought was "MY CHRISTMAS PARTY IS TODAY!!!" But could he get everything ready in time?

First, he finished decorating his treehouse.
He was REALLY INTO HOLIDAY DECORATING.

Next came the party food.
Luckily, Clark showed up to help.

While they were putting sprinkles on the cookies,
Chico saw the kitty cat crew coming up the trail.
"The guests are arriving," he said. "We have to hurry!!"

Clark filled his trunk with sprinkles and finished
the last cookies all at once. "DONE!!"

Chico dashed to his room and put on his special holiday tool belt.

confetti blaster
stuffie brusher
Christmas crackers
candy crusher
bobtail ringer
chocolate chopper
kooky cutter
lollipopper
a bunch of batteries

jumbo tape roll
purple crayon
mitten scraper
sparkle spray-on
candy cane
hog mixers
present pryers
small-toy fixers
all-time favorite scissors

He ran to the front door.

He flipped on the party lights.

He was ready!

He looked out onto his yard, and this is what he saw:

All his friends were arriving with gifts and FOOD!

The Big Bug Band unloaded
their sleds and began to play.

The cookie bar was
twelve feet long!

There was a light-up
cocoa fountain

and a Christmas tree
made of burritos.

PLUCK

The mega-cheese ball was
a big hit with the rodents.

There was a ball pit
filled with candy.

On the deck was an ice cream
snowman with a suitcase of Popsicles.

There was a candy cane
tunnel in the backyard.

The cocoa cream
yule log was the size
of an actual log!

Chico's hard work had paid off.
The party was a hit!

Soon it was time for Chico to give out presents.

They all gathered around the fireplace to open them.

Everyone went wild!
They loved their gifts!!

Everyone hugged Chico and thanked him, and they gave him presents too: tools, a book, mittens, building toys, and at least seven pairs of fuzzy socks.

Clark gave him a Banana bobsled.

"The Banana Splitter I've always wanted!!
Thank you, Clark!" said Chico.

"Thank YOU, Chico!" said Clark, strumming a
few bars on his new electric guitar. "You sure
are good at fixing AND MAKING things!"

I LOVE IT!

Clark did a dance
move and fell
into the ball pit.

Everyone cheered and raised their glasses of punch.

CHEERS!

The band began to play "Jingle Bells." They all danced and sang along late into the night.

"This is the best Christmas ever!" said Chico.

And everybody agreed that it was!